NORTH AMERICAN DUCKS, GEESE AND SWANS

Ruth Soffer

DOVER PUBLICATIONS, INC.
New York

Bibliographical Note

North American Ducks, Geese and Swans Coloring Book is a new work, first published by Dover Publications, Inc., in 1996.

International Standard Book Number
ISBN-13: 978-0-486-29165-9
ISBN-10: 0-486-29165-0

Manufactured in the United States by Courier Corporation
29165007   2014
www.doverpublications.com

PUBLISHER'S NOTE

NO BIRDS ASSOCIATED with water are better known than waterfowl — the ducks, geese and swans. The majesty of the Mute Swan may be witnessed on ponds around the world. Common Eiders keep us warm with eiderdown. The noble form and distinct voice of Canada Geese as they pass overhead in well-known "V" formation reminds us of crisp autumn mornings. Mallards, the best known of all ducks, have learned to beg for food in many a neighborhood park pond around the world — and to keep their distance wherever they are hunted!

There are about 150 species of swans, geese and ducks, all belonging to the biological order of Anseriformes, or waterfowl. At least some waterfowl are found on every continent except Antarctica. Ducks are the largest of the three groups, and they may also be subdivided into at least two major groups, the dabbling ducks and the diving ducks. The best known dabbling duck is the Mallard. Perhaps the best known diving duck, at least in the United States, is the Canvasback. Dabblers, also known as puddle ducks, tend to be found in shallower water. They feed by tipping forward, with their tails in the air. Only on rare occasions do they dive beneath the surface for their food. Diving ducks, on the other hand, usually feed by diving entirely beneath the surface.

In this book you will find 44 drawings showing 43 kinds of waterfowl. Two of the drawings show other birds that are sometimes associated with waterfowl, although they are unrelated: the Common Loon, a stately inhabitant of northern lakes, and the Northern Gannet, seen offshore in the winter along the East Coast.

Fifteen of the drawings are shown in color on the covers. The general coloration of all of the birds is indicated in the captions. This information may be supplemented by consulting any of the popular field guides to birds (most if not all of the birds in this book will be found in guides to the birds of North America).

The drawings of the birds are arranged in taxonomic order — that is, based on considerations of anatomy and evolution.

Alphabetical lists of common and of scientific names may be found at the end of the book.

Tundra Swan (*Cygnus columbianus*). Once called the Whistling Swan in North America, the Tundra Swan nests on the tundra of the far north of Alaska and Canada. Like the other North American swans, it is almost all white.

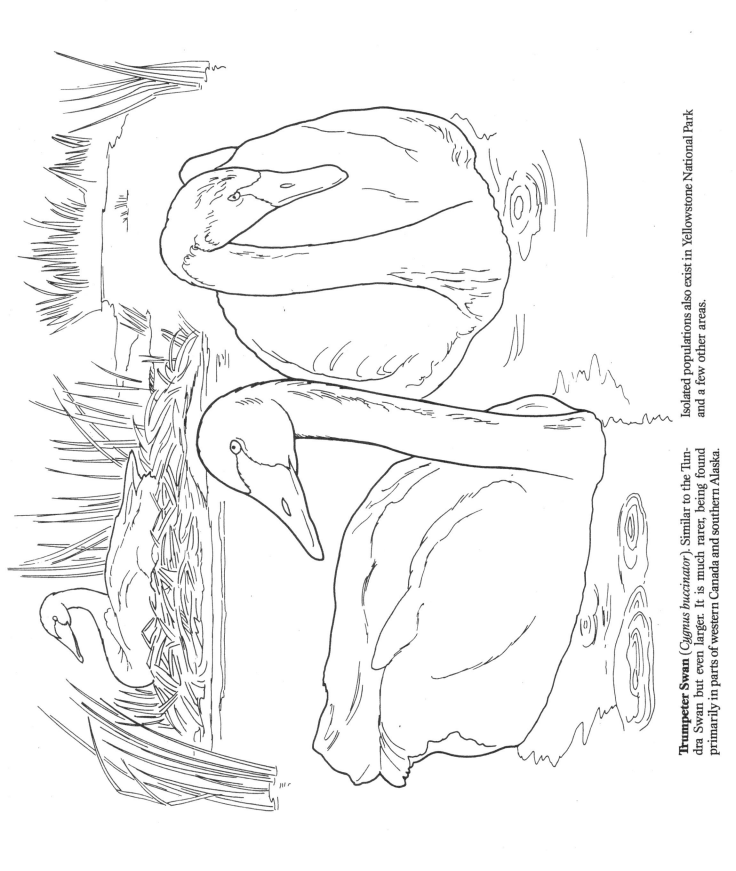

Trumpeter Swan (*Cygnus buccinator*). Similar to the Tundra Swan but even larger. It is much rarer, being found primarily in parts of western Canada and southern Alaska. Isolated populations also exist in Yellowstone National Park and a few other areas.

5

Mute Swan (*Cygnus olor*). This most familiar swan with its gracefully curved neck is an import to North America (and elsewhere) from the Old World, well known from many a local park pond. In parts of the northeast United States it has established breeding populations.

Greater White-fronted Goose (*Anser albifrons*). A gray-brown goose of moderate size found only in isolated areas of Western North America. The white patch around its bill gives it its name.

Snow Goose (Blue Goose) (*Chen caerulescens*). Most Snow Geese are white with black wings but there is a variant that is largely brownish black (retaining a white head and neck). Once considered a different species, this variant is still frequently called the "Blue Goose."

Ross' Goose (*Chen rossii*). In the eastern United States, a Ross' Goose is on rare occasions seen in a flock of Snow Geese. Otherwise this uncommon bird is found only in a few parts of the West. It looks like a smaller version of the Snow Goose.

Emperor Goose (*Chen canagica*). Seen mostly in Western Alaska and the Aleutian Islands but strays as far south as California. Its white head and black throat and chin are distinctive.

Canada Goose (*Branta canadensis*). This is simply the best-known goose in North America, found almost everywhere north of Mexico. It is not universally loved, however, having a habit of taking up residence on golf courses, fouling the grass and generally making life miserable for the golfers.

Brant (*Branta bernicla*). Relatively few people are familiar with this black-brown-and-white seagoing relative of the Canada Goose. While not rare, its wintering population is highly concentrated in a few areas along the East and West Coasts. In the summer even fewer people get to see it, as it breeds in the far north.

Barnacle Goose (*Branta leucopsis*). Occasionally seen in eastern Canada, the Barnacle Goose breeds in Greenland. It is a sea goose like the Brant, but it tends to feed further inland. Similar in appearance to its close relatives the Brant and Canada Goose, the Barnacle Goose is distinguished by the hoodlike pattern on its head.

Mallard (*Anas platyrhynchos*). The male Mallard's green head and brown breast separated by a white stripe are better known than the colors of any other water bird in the Northern Hemisphere. This very familiar dabbling duck has also been introduced in parts of the Southern Hemisphere. As with many ducks, the female looks very different, being mostly a speckled brown.

14

American Black Duck (*Anas rubripes*). This duck of eastern North America is so closely related to the Mallard that the two species frequently hybridize. Looking like darker female Mallards, both sexes of the Black Duck are uncharacteristically very close in appearance. Unlike most Mallards, Black Ducks are very shy and will fly off at the approach of humans.

Gadwall (*Anas strepera*). This handsome relative of Mallards and Black Ducks is found throughout the United States and southern Canada. It is the only dabbling duck to show a white "speculum" – a wing patch that consists of most of the secondary flight feathers. The male also has jet-black tail coverts (the feathers just above and below the tail).

Green-winged Teal (*Anas crecca*). This is the smallest dabbling duck in North America. Another race of this species also inhabits Europe and Asia. The male Green-winged Teal has a beautiful chestnut head with bright green facial patches.

American Wigeon (*Anas americana*). The distinctive white head patch of the male American Wigeon has led to the hunters' nickname of "Baldpate." It is commonest along the East and West Coasts in the Winter, and inland and further to the north in breeding season.

Northern Pintail (*Anas acuta*). Among the most beautiful ducks in North America, the male Northern Pintail has a chocolate brown head and very long black tail. The white on the breast extends upward in thin stripes on either side of the head. Much more common in the West than the East.

Northern Shoveler (*Anas clypeata*). Common throughout North America (more so in the West), the Northern Shoveler is the only North American duck besides the Mallard of which the male has a bright green head. The shoveler also has a distinctive spatulate (spoonlike) bill that helps it filter food from the bottom of the muddy ponds it frequents.

20

Blue-winged Teal (*Anas discors*). The white crescent on the bluish gray cheek of the male Blue-winged Teal immediately identifies this lovely bird. Both sexes have a light blue patch on the forewing. Found in much of North America but more common in the East.

Cinnamon Teal (*Anas cyanoptera*). Closely related to the Blue-winged Teal, this dabbler is found only in the West. The male has a rich cinnamon-colored head, neck and flanks.

Ruddy Duck (*Oxyura jamaicensis*). This chunky diving duck is not closely related to any other duck of this continent except the very rare Masked Duck. It is awkward both in flight and on land, spending most of its time in the water, where it feeds chiefly on underwater vegetation.

23

Fulvous Whistling-Duck (*Dendrocygna bicolor*). This and the next species are members of the small group of Whistling-Ducks (formerly called Tree Ducks, though only some perch in trees). Somewhat gooselike, these birds feed on land and in the water, sometimes diving for their food. This species is found primarily in south Texas, Louisiana and Florida.

Black-bellied Whistling-Duck (*Dendrocygna autumnalis*). Similar to the previous species, this bird is distinguished by its red bill and black belly. The sexes of Whistling-Ducks tend to have the same or at least very similar coloration. The Black-bellied Whistling-Duck is found only in very restricted areas in south Texas and Arizona, although it occasionally strays into other states.

Wood Duck (*Aix sponsa*). Many consider the multicolored Wood Duck the most beautiful duck in North America. Aptly named, this unusual waterfowl prefers woodlands. It nests in holes in trees (or artificial nest boxes where available) and often perches in trees.

Canvasback (*Aythya valisineria*). A favorite with hunters because its vegetable diet gives it sweet-tasting flesh, the well-known Canvasback is also a beautiful bird. The male's head is a rich chestnut, contrasting with a black breast and tail and white sides. The female is colored in different shades of brown.

Redhead (*Aythya americana*). Similar to the Canvasback, the Redhead is identified by its more rounded head and shorter bill. Like the Canvasback it is found in marshes, ponds and lakes throughout much of North America, though more commonly west of the Mississippi.

Ring-necked Duck (*Aythya collaris*). The cinnamon ring around the neck of this marsh and woodland duck is hard to see. This bird is more readily identified by the ring around the bill. The male's head has a gloss of purple. The female is mostly brown.

Greater Scaup (*Aythya marila*). Common principally on the coasts, this diving duck is often found in bays in the colder months. Its breeding range is the far north of Canada and Alaska. Similar in appearance to the Lesser Scaup, it may be distinguished by the more rounded head and the greenish gloss on the head of the male. The female has a white facial patch around her bill.

Lesser Scaup (*Aythya affinis*). This duck has a broader breeding range than the similar Greater Scaup, being found on small ponds in the lower 48 states. In winter, when it is most likely to be seen together with the Greater Scaup, the male can be distinguished by the purple gloss on its slightly pointier head.

Common Eider (*Somateria mollissima*). This is the best-known of the eiders, all of which, even in winter, inhabit the icy waters of the North, from which their covering of down helps insulate them. Common Eiders are readily identified by their sloping forehead. The males have a lovely black-white-and-greenish coloration.

King Eider (*Somateria spectabilis*). The male's head is very different from that of the Common Eider, with a yellow-orange-and-black protruding patch over the bill and a blue crown. These contrast with greenish-tinged white cheeks, white foreparts and extensive areas of black. King Eiders are more irregularly distributed and may sometimes stray far from their usual range.

Spectacled Eider (*Somateria fischeri*). Although it breeds in North America (and elsewhere), few people ever see this lovely bird, for its nesting grounds are on coastal tundra in the north and west of Alaska and in Siberia. And unlike some of its cousins, it does not visit more populous areas at other times but winters out in the middle of the Bering Sea, where it may be seen only in such places as the remote Pribilof Islands.

Steller's Eider (*Polysticta stelleri*). A denizen of the frozen North like its distant cousin the Spectacled Eider, this bird is much easier to see. It winters off the coast of southern Alaska and may be seen around some of the most populous sections at that time. It is also found in northeastern Asia. The male is very distinctive, with a greenish patch on his crown as well as a black eye ring and throat.

White-winged Scoter (*Melanitta fusca*). A number of ducks are found off both coasts of the U.S. and Canada and rarely inland on fresh water except in the breeding season. These are the sea ducks, all of them diving ducks that eat a variety of oceanic animal and vegetable matter. Some of these ducks are the scoters, of which the White-winged Scoter is distinguished by the white patch found on the wings of both sexes.

Surf Scoter (*Melanitta perspicillata*). The Surf Scoter has the most unusual bill among the scoters: orange, white and black in the male. Females are identified by white patches before and behind the eyes. In winter this bird is seen as far south as the tip of Baja California.

Harlequin Duck (*Histrionicus histrionicus*). The combination of gray-blue, black, rust and white hues on the plumage of the male of this unusual duck is impossible to describe adequately. It is generally harder to find than the scoters, preferring rocky shores. It also does not winter as far south, most birds flying down only as far as northern California in the West and New England in the East.

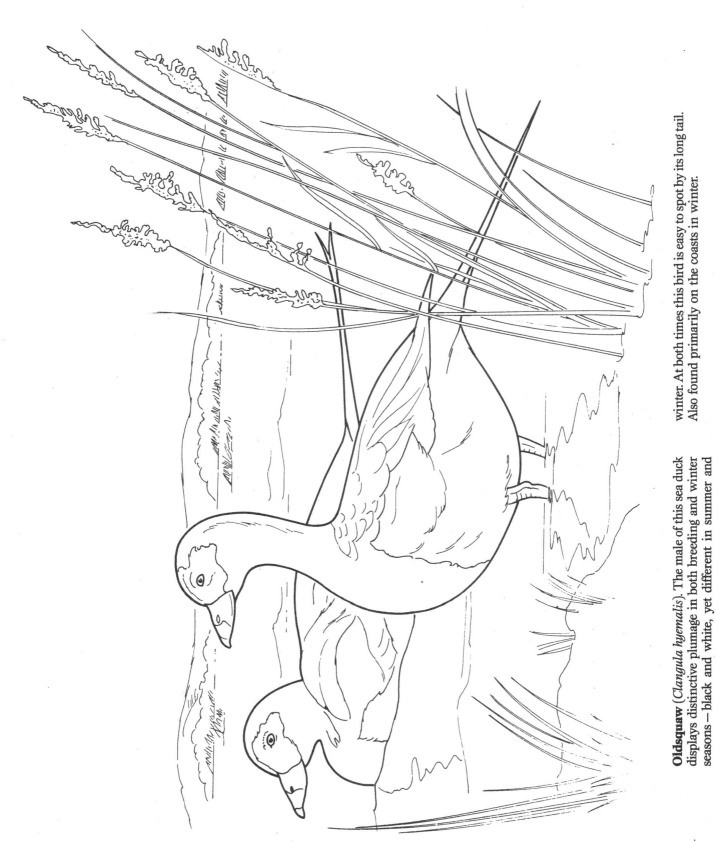

Oldsquaw (*Clangula hyemalis*). The male of this sea duck displays distinctive plumage in both breeding and winter seasons — black and white, yet different in summer and winter. At both times this bird is easy to spot by its long tail. Also found primarily on the coasts in winter.

Barrow's Goldeneye (*Bucephala islandica*) and **Common Goldeneye** (*Bucephala clangula*). The goldeneyes and bufflehead form a distinct group of their own. Of them, the hardest to find is Barrow's Goldeneye (represented in this drawing by the two ducks in the foreground), being found primarily in the northeast and especially northwest corners of the United States and adjoining Canada. The aptly named Common Goldeneye (the male of which is seen in a typical courting posture, upper left, with the female next to him) winters not only along the coast but also inland in much of the United States. The male Barrow's Goldeneye has a white crescent on a purplish face, the Common a round white spot on a greenish face.

Bufflehead (*Bucephala albeola*). This chunky little diving duck was aptly nicknamed "Butterball" by hunters. It may be found on fresh or saltwater in the colder months throughout most of the United States and Canada and parts of Mexico. The male is readily identified by the large white patch on an otherwise black head.

41

Common Merganser (*Mergus merganser*). The mergansers form yet another subgroup of diving ducks. These all have long bills with serrated edges suitable for grasping the fish that form the bulk of their diet. The Common Merganser is a large, handsome bird found over most of North America. The male's head is bright green; the female's head, which has a crest, is rust-colored.

Red-breasted Merganser (*Mergus serrator*). This merganser, slightly smaller than the Common, is mostly confined to the coasts of the United States and parts of Canada in the winter. Both sexes have crested heads. The female is similar to the female Common Merganser; the male has a green head and a noticeable broad white ring around its neck.

43

Hooded Merganser (*Lophodytes cucullatus*). This small merganser is less common than the others but more likely to be found in the United States in breeding season. The male's plumage, in particular, shows a striking pattern of black, white and rust. Both sexes have crested heads.

Northern Shelduck (*Tadorna tadorna*). This Eurasian species is found in many zoos and private waterfowl collections throughout North America. The male is readily identified by the knob at the base of his bill. He has a green head and neck and a rust-colored band across his chest.

Common Loon (*Gavia immer*). This well-known water bird breeds in Canada, Alaska and the northern extremes of the lower 48 states. Its yodeling calls create an eerie effect around wooded lakes. Though sometimes mistaken for a duck, it belongs to an entirely different order of birds.

Northern Gannet (*Sula bassanus*). This bird, totally unrelated to the ducks, also has completely different behavior and is not likely to be mistaken for any kind of waterfowl. Gannets are found only in, over and around saltwater. They breed in huge colonies on rocky cliffs in eastern Canada. In winter they move south along the East Coast and are often seen from shore far out at sea making spectacular plummeting dives for fish. The black-tipped white wings and white body are easily seen at a distance. Occasionally they will fly over land and then the rusty shade on the head of adult birds may be seen.

ALPHABETICAL LIST OF COMMON NAMES

ALPHABETICAL LIST OF SCIENTIFIC NAMES